First published in the United States of America in 2022 by Chronicle Books LLC.

Originally published in Japan in 2015 under the title *Riyu Ga Arimasu* by PHP Institute, Inc.

English translation rights arranged with PHP Institute, Inc., through Compass Rose LLC.

Text and illustrations copyright © 2015 by Shinsuke Yoshitake.

Original English translation © 2021 by PHP Institute, Inc.

English translation copyright © 2022 by Chronicle Books LLC.

Library of Congress Cataloging-in-Publication Data available.

ISBN 978-1-7972-1690-4

Manufactured in China.

Typeset in Minou.
Design by albireo, Inc.
Prepress: alema.
The illustrations in this book were rendered in pen and digitally.

10 9 8 7 6 5 4 3 2 1

Chronicle Books LLC
680 Second Street
San Francisco, California 94107

Chronicle Books—we see things differently. Become part of our community at www.chroniclekids.com.

I CAN EXPLAIN

Shinsuke Yoshitake

chronicle books · san francisco

I have a habit of picking my nose.
My mom always gets mad at me for it.
She says it's "bad manners."

Maybe if I just had an explanation,
it would be okay for me to pick my nose.

There's a button at the
back of my nose.

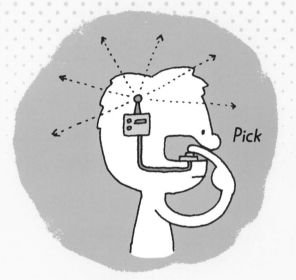

Pick

If I keep pressing the button,
my brain releases lots of
cheerful beams.

Pick
Pick
Pick

These beams have the power to put everyone in a good mood.

Okay, got it.

Click

Chew . . .

Ah! Now you're biting your nails!

Not exactly!
I'm–well, I'm . . .

When I bite my nails, I make a sound
that's inaudible to adults.

It makes the crows that hover around
the trash bags go away.

Oh, all right.
But there aren't any crows around at this time of day,
so you don't have to make any more of those sounds.

Okay, got it.

Shake shake shake

I'm not "shaking my legs."

I'm speaking the language of the moles.
I'm telling them about my day!

When I spill my food everywhere,

it's because some strange little creatures
are asking me to share with them.

And when I can't sit still,

Rustle

it's because I'm dealing with an ill-tempered chair
in the restaurant or classroom.

When I jump on my bed,

it's because I'm training for the possibility of the road turning into a trampoline. That way, I'll still be able to get to school!

When I run in the halls or in a store,

it's because there's a Dash Bug on top of my head,
and it makes my body move by itself.

When I climb on things,

it's because I'm training for when I find a cat stuck in a tree.

That way, I'll be able to save it.

When I make bubbles with my straw,

I'm actually making the universal sign for
"There's a lot going on, but I'm still okay."

When I chew my straw,

it's because I want to participate in the
International Straw Chewing Contest,

win first place,

use the prize money to build a boat,

and then take everyone on a trip around the world!

When I wipe my dirty hands on my pants or other clothes,

it's because I'd feel bad if I wiped my hands on
flowers, polar bears, or swans.

When I don't want to put on my pajamas even though
I've been out of the bath for a while,

it's because I'm training for the possibility of an evil alien
coming to my school and vacuuming up my clothes.
I'll be able to resist, even if I'm naked!

When I pick up random objects and bring them home,

What about this?

Ah!
That might work!

I'm actually helping to repair a broken alien spaceship.
I'm looking for parts that might be useful.

See?
I can explain everything!

Okay, I see.
I think I understand.

But can you at least try to be a little
more mindful of having good manners?

Okay, got it.

Great.

But even adults do things without realizing they're doing them, right?

Yeah, that's right.

For instance, you're always touching your hair like that, but why?

Um . . . like this?

Um . . . this is . . .

I know!

At the ends of my hair, there
are lots of meal ideas.

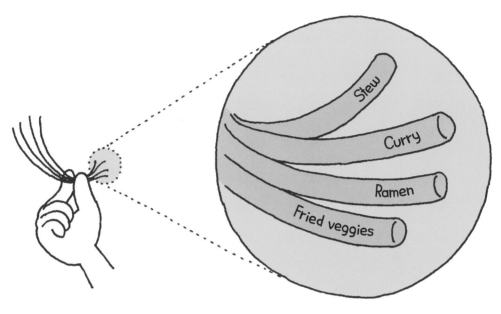

When it's time to prepare
dinner, I just choose a hair
to find out what to make.

So today is . . .